C000069274

Merih Günay

Sweet Chocolate

Sweet Chocolate

© 2021 Merih Günay

Translated from Turkish by Stuart Kline

ISBN 978-3-949197-52-9

Texianer Verlag

TuningenDeutschland

www.texianer.com

The finest moment of life is when you give up everything and actually start believing you are someone who is connected to life.

Balzac

The sun was just starting to rise over the city as they went out of the door of the apartment. They began walking up the hill from the bottom of the dark, narrow street. With a beaming smile on her face, the young woman clasped the man's arm. The night had ended for a few drunks staggering down from the top of the hill and who were bidding each other 'Good Morning' as they shuffled off down their side streets. Arm in arm, the couple climbed the slope in silence for a few minutes and after they had come out into the old square, disappeared amongst the vehicles on that frosty November morning.

13 years ago

The man murmured, "God loves me!" while looking at the computer monitor on the table where he sat. The young girl turned her gaze to the man's face and waited for him to continue.

"These were texts I wrote piece by piece at different times," he said, looking towards her face.

"Now they're starting to come together." A sincere smile appeared on the girl's face. "Independent texts I wrote in different years are now complementing each other, do you understand where I'm going from?"

The girl expressed she understood with a shy nod.

A year ago

You already read the last story I wrote, I didn't even write a line since then. I don't think I'll be able to write anymore. You know, I came down with a severe bout of tuberculosis shortly after you left. Anyway, that was our last dialogue with you,

"I've come down with tuberculosis."

"You should get some rest now."

Neither the natural effect of the illness nor the heavy medication put my mind at ease. There's constant discomfort, anxiety and fear hanging over me. It's not good for writing, nor is it for living. He continued writing,

"I'm really glad to see you again."

"I'm glad to see you again, too⋯"

7

"I looked everywhere online for you, and it looks like your account was closed down, too. I also sent a lot of e-mails to your old address, but they came back every time."

"Yeah, I closed my accounts after I got married. I looked for you a lot, there were a few accounts, but I didn't want to write without being sure they were yours or not."

"You know, I wasn't using them. I'm not into social media very much. I don't like how technology is advancing so quickly."

"I know. I remember how you didn't even use a cellphone."

"I still don't use one, except for the line the company gave me. I've been walking from home to work and back every day since the commuter train line stopped running, something like six or seven years now. I put in about nine kilometers on foot every day."

"Yes, the trains don't run anymore. I was really sad when I heard about that."

"Do you remember how I ran into you on the train one morning?"

"Yes, of course I remember."

"You were a dazzling young girl back then, and now you've become a very beautiful woman."

9 months ago

AT THE INN

Conversation with a salt shaker

He started the conversation by saying, "Tonight... My Dear Friend the reason why I'm here is..." he paused, glancing to his left and his right. He cleared his throat after making sure nobody was watching him, adjusted his vocal tone and went on,

"My mother's death."

"If my mother hadn't died today, if I wasn't forced to go outside my shell for the first time in all those years, if I didn't have to ride in the passenger seat of the ambulance last night at midnight, if I didn't go from hospital to hospital... I wouldn't be here tonight, because I haven't loved in a long time."

He took a break, asking the salt shaker to let him fill his raki glass. Then he lit his cigarette, took a deep drag on it, then continued,

"I don't love."

There was silence. He and the salt shaker gazed at each other for what seemed an eternity. He was the one who broke the silence once more, this time in a different tone of voice,

"You don't love either, do you?" he said.

He preferred not to strongly emphasize the end of his sentence. It was stern but naive as well.

He was going to continue saying, "If you had loved," but the siren of a fire truck passing outside kept him from doing so. Although he made an effort to do so, he couldn't concentrate and went silent.

He was totally drunk when he arrived home. He got undressed without turning on the lights and just sat there for a while. Then he turned his head where he was sitting, looked towards his computer and reached over to touch the on/off button.

He sat in his armchair and waited for the monitor to come on. He lit another cigarette.

She was there.

He first looked at her name, then at her photo. She had changed very little. Maybe just her hair, it was longer and darker. She had said, "It's a lighter color during the summer. Maybe that's why."

He glanced at the clock. He thought maybe she appeared online even if he might not be at her computer. Then again, unable to hold back, he wrote her,

"Hello, could we chat for a bit, when you're free, maybe tomorrow?"

He wanted to write that he'd had a terrible day with the salt shaker, the ambulance, the coffin, his hair—but the words knotted up in his throat when he read her reply on the screen.

"I'm always free for you."

Five in the morning

Darkness. She's on the bed... Her petite body has been slowly rising and falling on me for nearly half an hour... I watch her face. It's sweaty, flushed. Her dreamy, drunken eyes... Her hair is scattered all around, the frizzy bits are drifting into my eyes, nose and lips. Her soft, dark, brown hair dances on my face. She's smiling. As she smiles, her lips broaden and cover her entire face. She's drenched in her nightgown. As she moves over me, she softly pumps my chest with her small hands. I'm watching, it's five o'clock in the morning. Love is sweaty...

She

She's vivacious. She's constantly talking. She's laughing her head off at times when she's not talking. She's talking, she's laughing and wandering about. She's always moving, flittering to and fro. She's making me dizzy. Following her wearies out my rusty mind. How old is she? She looks quite young on the screen. I've rotted out and I stink.

So, there's a heart, a glass, followed by a kiss. Then another heart. Is there something I don't get?

And to see me, of all things. After all these years. "But," I said, "If you come..." Even if you come and if we meet..." she didn't let me finish what I was saying,

"You can do whatever you please."

20 years ago

From the good old days

We were sitting on stools in front of the bar on the mezzanine floor. Emilia and I. Ekrem, if I remember his name correctly, was the barman standing opposite us and was polishing up glasses with a cloth in his hand. Night had fallen and we were drinking beer and watching the rain pour down in the dark outside from the wide windows encircling the bar. How many beers, our tenth, fifteenth, twentieth, we weren't keeping track. Once in awhile, I'd turn towards Emilia and say,

"Hey, it's raining." Smiling as she rotated the large glass between her palms, she replied,

"Larisa hasn't come yet, either," as we laughed together. Silence reigned supreme around us as there wasn't anybody on the bar floor but us. From time to time, Emilia gently sang Bregoviç songs played on the cassette deck and she moved her shoulders to the rhythm.

We agreed with a beautiful Russian girl named Larisa, whom I had met that day around noon in the breakfast hall, to meet up that evening in the bar. I thought we could eat something, chat, get drunk, and have a nice night, and I told Emilia that. She said, "Fine, I'll get up when she arrives." Emilia was a beautiful woman, with short blonde hair, a slim waist, and nearly 5'10". We'd known each other for a few years and she'd come around every couple of months, sometimes staying over a night, sometimes two. She was married to Admir, was lovers with Sasha but had no children from either one of her partners.

"Emilia!"

"Yes?"

"It's raining."

"Larisa hasn't come either."

Meanwhile, Ekrem has refilled our glasses and we have a good laugh and it's raining ever more intensely outside.

"The rain was expected to let up in some places."

The music volume rose inexplicably as the time passed,

> *"Nemavisesunca*
> *Nema visemeseca*
> *Nema tebe nema mene*
> *Nicegvise nema joj"*

When Larisa appeared at the stairway, going up to the bar holding an umbrella, Emilia got up slowly from her stool and took her room key from the counter. She leaned over to my ear as she passed behind me and whispered,

"You have a nice life, my friend." Just then, the air sprung to life with Emilia's and Larisa's mingling scents. I grinned.

I murmured, "Eh, it's not bad."

12 years ago

Upon lifting his head after a brief coughing fit, his squinting eyes caught the orange flames of the gas stove leaning against the wall. As his coughing attack persisted, those flames turned from orange to blue, as warm sweat pouring from his hair drenched the pillowcase and sheets. He was turning over and over in his bed like a rotisserie, muttering vaguely. The room didn't seem real to him. It was as if the various wispy smoke shapes emerging from the flames had scattered around the bed frame and were trying to coax him out of bed. He was trying to stop the spittle sputtering from his mouth with one hand while chasing the smoke signals with his other.

In his dream

(Sanatorium)

His hair was long and filthy, his body doubled over, his thoughts blurred, his eyes pale. He didn't know how old he was. He had no family, no home, no Hope (Bob), no Cash (Johnny) and no Jobs (Steve). He was Mr. Bojangles. He went to sleep wherever he found it convenient to sleep, ate whatever food he found convenient to eat, cleaning it using tree leaves. People moved away from him out of sheer fear, animals moved away from his putrid stench. Kids not only fled him, they rained rocks upon him. That's because he'd been neither a good boy, nor a good student, nor a good worker. He was the spitting image of Mr. Bojangles. His shapeless face was not sad, nor was it cheerful. It was neither black nor white. There were stains on his face, his hands and in the exposed parts of his half-torn suit.

The kids dragged him about, shouting and stoning him as they went. He was spinning where he was, with his head in his hands. He spun to the spinning sounds of Dylan's 'Everyone Must Get Stoned,' as dogs barked around the kids who were throwing rocks around him. When in fact, he didn't appreciate noise. What's more, Mr. Bojangles didn't appreciate being stoned and he didn't appreciate well-dressed people and fattened animals. He didn't appreciate houses, furniture or cars. He was fond of food that was tossed out in the garbage, he was fond of the rain and rats, too. Water would fill rat nests if the rain fell long and heavy. In such situations, they'd all rise to the surface, and invade villages en masse when it got dark outside. He followed them on all fours, watching them as they pillaged food, warehouses, and clothes. Then came the owls, the night predators. They'd silently dive on their necks and swallow the mice up in one fell swoop. The rain would swallow the rats' nests, the rats would swallow up people's food, and the owls would swallow up the rats with full bellies. Later, when the mice, snakes and owls all retreated back to their nests, the villagers would come out and stone the heck out of him. Because he had never been a good child, a good husband, a good father. Sometimes he'd just loiter about, other times he'd run away. Sometimes his stomach would be full, while he'd go hungry most of the time. He ate little, slept even less and never talked. On some nights noise would get into his ears. It was neither the sound of birds, nor horses, nor thunder. It was neither the sound of an ant clambering through his hair, nor a dog trying to snap its chain, nor the sound of leaves swaying in the breeze. Sounds came from the days of yore and from lands far away.

Grasshoppers would hop right into his ears on nights when sounds didn't. On those nights, Bojangles would put his ear to the ground and patiently wait for the grasshopper to emerge. Upon the grasshopper's emergence, Bojangles would nab it and nibble on it like a snack. Those times it didn't emerge, he'd sleep well as no other sound would come into his ears. All his teeth were rotted, as he had eaten raw meat for years. Scraggily toothed Bojangles endeavored to look for another place that had few rocks, kids and dogs. Long, grungy haired, hunchbacked, fuzzy thinking, and pale eyed Bojangles, proceeding on four legs, occasionally raising his head to sniff the air, snapping at grasshoppers he encountered along the way. The sounds of ironmongery, tin clanking, and clarinets blowing came from the villages he passed. There was also the smells of copper, garbage, food.

An Escape Attempt

(the recent past)

"Look sweetheart ⋯"

I was astounded, I was nervous and I guess I understood correctly what had transpired.

"We hadn't seen each other in quite a long time."

I didn't know how I was going to pick up the pieces, and I wanted to skip on out of there. Basically, to save my ass without screwing everything up even more.

"I'm not the man you remember. Those days are a long time ago."

She was waiting without interrupting. I knew that. She was looking at my words on her telephone screen, smiling and waiting for me to finish. I was kind of hoping she'd cut in and say what was on her mind, but I went on when I noticed nothing was coming from her end.

"I'm thinking of the good old days." That was ridiculous. I shouldn't have written that.

"Yes, I sometimes think of them, in fact, I perhaps always live in the past."

Why isn't she writing anything?

(The very near past)

"You say you're going to come here to see me. Well, this is going to be a bit heavy on me. For instance, I haven't ridden in any sort of vehicle in years. Like I mentioned before, I even walk to and from work everyday. In the snow, in the rain, in the cold. That's because I don't see anyone. I don't want to talk with anyone and don't want to get close to anyone. In fact, I don't even want to live. I mean, if you come, I can't meet you, I can't wander around with you. What if we don't see each other and just write like this once in a while, I mean, wouldn't it be better?"

I waited for her reply. She's reading what I'm writing but she wasn't intervening, just waiting for me to finish. How should I finish? I took a deep breath and continued.

"I can't take you anywhere, I couldn't even if I wanted to. I'm rotten to the core. Don't you understand me?"

Why should she understand? She's full of life. She's young, good-looking, successful, and happy. "I mean, sweetheart, I'm telling you I'm even having a hard time staying on my feet."

Come on, let's finish this off. Strike the final blow, get her off the line straightaway, "If I have a hard time just keeping on my feet, I can't have you by my side."

Once again, she managed to knock me out of my mind with a single sentence. A sentence that was so concise, so strong, so cordial, so full of love, it hurt my eyes just reading it,

"I'd do everything for you."

(Seems like yesterday)

"Why did you wait so long to write to me?"

"You were so wrapped up in yourself that I didn't want to poke you. Speaking of poking, don't get me wrong, if I woke you up, you probably wouldn't have noticed me anyway. I mean, what do you think, I wasn't going to find you if I wanted to? I waited for the right time. I have no new feelings for you. I've had them all since the first moment I saw you, maybe from even before then, from other lives, you know what I mean?"

"In that case, maybe it would've been better had we started way back then."

"Why?"

"Maybe I wouldn't have become sick, I wouldn't have stopped writing, and I wouldn't have left my jobs."

"Darling, all this should've been experienced. We're evolving. The things you went through, the things I went through. Everything's alright, and is going the way it should."

"Great, you're coming to me then."

"I'm here darling. I really wanted to be at your side in those days as well."

An ordinary day in the past

The girl's name was Oksana. She lived in the same room as me for about six months. I should say she loved me like crazy. After making love at night, I'd turn my back and fall sleep. I'd find her watching me with swollen eyes when I awoke in the morning. One day, a friend of hers by the name of Marina came around. She had long black hair and wore a 90 bra. They were good friends. We stayed in the same room for about three months and starting from the first night while we were destroying vodka, Marina was in my lap when Oksana went into the bathroom. I didn't understand how it happened. She didn't either.

"But Oksana is my friend," she said.

"So what, she's my lover too!" I replied."

Oksana was really loyal to me. She was also really tight friends with Marina. For that reason, I first slept with Oksana that night. When I woke up in the morning, Marina was in my embrace. She was a fine woman, with long, black hair and a number 90 bra.

Quite recently

"You've had a lot of relationships, darling, and a lot of loves. There were a lot of good years. This was your respite period, think of it like that."

"A jubilee."

"Yeah, that's it. The years abandoned to rest and relaxation."

"Fine, so what about now?"

"It'll be the way you want again, it's already that way. You'll love, you'll write, you'll continue life right where you left off."

"So what about you?"

"For all intents and purposes, I belong to you, darling."

15 years ago

I should've been hungry, but I didn't feel like eating. It was five o'clock. I was waiting impatiently for another hour to pass. That's when I was going to happily spend the remainder of the day reunited with my bottles. What did Nora say on the telephone? She wasn't going to be home tonight, but she cooked me some food and left it for me to eat. Wonderful. So, what did she make? *Mousaka, with a pilaf on the side.* That's fine, but was there any bread, too? *There was a little left over from yesterday.*

Another five minutes passed. Time was ticking away interminably between the hours of five and six. Why was that? *That's when desires began in the body and patience was whittled away.* What about the consciousness? *That's too much for it to know. Besides, it doesn't want to know.*

I'm glad there's mousaka. He can heat it up with the pilaf and eat it when he gets home. Then he can go to sleep. Today's the weekend, what if he rewards himself before six? *No way, then the discipline is ruined.* What about your body? *He doesn't know and perhaps it's all in the mind.* What did the doctor say? *"If you continue like this, we won't have any other suggestion other than to pray for you!"*

What if I don't drink for a while? *It'll be good for you.* In that case, let's get started by not drinking today, for instance. Fine, what shall we do instead of drinking? *You can watch television.* I don't watch television. *You can read a book.* I don't read books either. *You can go to the coffeehouse and play games.* I never go to the coffeehouse. *Then knock off early, go waltzing Matilda, then go home.* Sure.

The weather's fine. We closed the shop. Let's walk slowly. How about that, everyone's walking. *Great.* Most of them are going from the left. Why? *Because the shade is on the left side, that's why.* Fine, let's go over to the left as well. What time is it? *Five thirty.* What d'ya think, should we turn back? *Why?* The signs have started, my hands are trembling. *Don't worry about it, keep going.* Okay. *Look at that beautiful house.* Yeah, it's really nice. Mousaka, with pilaf on the side. Then I'll go and get some sleep. *Sure.* Maybe I'll watch some television, too. *You can watch.* Okay.

What time is it? *It's twenty to six.* Shall we head back? *Let's not turn back, let's keep on walking. If not, we can buy something near your house and drink at home.* Fine.

Hey, look at that kid, he's tugging on her bag. *What's the woman doing?* She's just noticed, and is trying to save her bag. The boy's hanging on tight, and the woman's shouting. *What's happening now?* People are now looking that way, the boy's dropped her bag, and he's fleeing. There's a cop car, it's in the nick of time, the kid's gone into a side street. *What about the people?* They're chasing him with the cops. *Are they going to catch him?* I don't know, maybe. What time is it? *It's ten 'til.* Shall we head back? *No, let's wait.* Why should we wait? *Are they going to catch the kid?* Okay, let's wait. I wonder if we have any yogurt too? Hey, look, here they come. *Did they catch him* Yes, they finally got hold of him. *Good for them. C'mon, let's go.*

Is it six yet? *No, not yet. How are your hands?* They're shaking like my grandma's. How long before we reach the house? We're almost there. *Pick up something from the dried fruit and nuts shop.* I don't like that stuff. *Pick up some fruit then.* I don't eat it. Are we there yet? *Yes, we're there.* Is it six yet? *Yes, it's even five past.* Let's crack open the windows, it's stuffy in here. *Open them.* Let's change our clothes and heat up our food. Did you see any yogurt in the fridge? *No.* Never mind then. The phone's ringing. *Just let it ring. Are you full?* Yes. *What are you going to do now?* I'm going to get some shuteye. *Fine.* I'm lying down, what time is it? *It's six thirty.* I'm going to get some sleep. *Are you sleepy?* No, I'm not. I shut my eyes. When I was small my mother used to tell me "count sheep," I'm going to count women. *So, count them.* They're lined up in a row, and passing one-by-one in front of my eyes. Look, there's Oraib. *The dark-skinned one?* Yes, and Yeliz's right behind her. *Wow, that's nice. You should count them naked.* Why's that? *So your mind doesn't get messed up.* Fine, have it your way. *How many have you counted so far?*

I got confused, I'm going to start all over, what time is it? *It's seven.* Good, I'm counting backwards. Seven, six, five, four, three—what if I drink a little? *No way, you couldn't control yourself.* You're right, how many pieces of bread did I eat? *Two.* Wasn't it one? *It was two slices.* What are they going to do to the kid? They let him go long ago. *Did you sleep? You didn't sleep.* Is it eight yet? *Not yet.* Why did you bring my mother to my mind? *I didn't bring her up, you did.*

I remember eating one piece. *Did you miss her?* No, I didn't like her very much. Isn't it eight yet? *I guess you're sleeping.* It's going to be bad if I get up at night. *Then don't get up, sleep.* Why did they let the kid go? *I don't know.* Did you lock the door? *Yes.*

I need to get up, I need a drink. *Okay.* I'm drinking water. *Are your innards burning?* Yes. *You're dripping it on the floor.* Can I look out of the window? *Look, it's already nine o'clock, you can go back to sleep soon.* Am I going to sleep? *You'll sleep.* Fine.

There are three corner shops on our street. *Where you going?* There are some things in the display case. *Hey! I thought you weren't going to drink?* Just a sip. *You promise?* Promise. *Fine.* They're not there, did you remove them? *No, I didn't.* They're not here either. *What are you going to do?* I'm getting dressed. *Why?* I want to get some stuff before the corner shops close. *If only you could endure a little longer.* Did you lock the door? *No, I didn't.* Where's the key? *I don't know.* What time is it?

It's nine thirty. I'm sleepy, I'm going to bed. *Okay, then.*

Fire trucks are racing. *Do you see the fire?* No, I just see them passing in front of me. *How many passed?* I couldn't count they were moving too fast. *What else do you see?* The engines have finished passing, now they're being followed by naked women. *Do you recognize them?* No. *There are ten.* I didn't do anything to anyone. *I know that.* Can you tuck me in? *Isn't it warm in here?* Tuck me in, I'm cold. *Fine.* Tell them I'm doing alright, have them open the door. *I'll tell them.* Say he's sleeping. *Okay, I will.*

Get these blankets off me, I'm burning up. *Hey, talk nice with me.* I'm not an evil person. *I know that.* They're knocking down the electrical poles. *Who?* I don't know, they're wearing blue overalls. Somebody's squirting water with a hose, and someone else is brushing it away. *Do you love them?* Not all the time. I regret it most of the time.

You sleep really nice. Am I sleeping? Would it be okay if I didn't go to school? *Okay, I won't wake you up.* I shoved him. *You said you didn't.* I was scared, his head hit the top of the steel rod. *If only you had informed someone, he might've been saved.* I fled the scene. *It's midnight now.* What happened to them? *To whom?* The naked women became little girls. *You're little too.* They're riding bikes. *What are you doing?* I have a pigeon in my hand and I'm washing him nicely. *How many are left.* There are three more posts, then it's going to finish and we'll be going home. *Okie dokie, artichokie.*

Is it six o'clock yet?

Yep.

The hour between five and six is absolute hell for me.

I know, I know.

Tranquility

"Don't think about anything, sweetheart," she said. "Don't get stressed out, I'm going to take care of everything."

Am I hallucinating again?

"I'm going to come to our agreed rendezvous spot and take you from there and I'll bring you back to the same place the day after. Just be there when I get there, and think about nothing else."

Isn't that just too much, why?

"I feel I have to repeat it, sweetheart. I hadn't been with anyone for years. I'm all alone in my tiny, simple, awful world. These things you say are too much for me."

I know she's going to surprise me again.

"Because you are putting up with all this, you always have loneliness, negativity, misery in your mind. If you change your thoughts, you can change your life. Do you want to smoke, you can smoke as much as you want. Do you want to wander around drunk all day long, do so. Do you want to be a maverick, be one. It doesn't matter to me. Regardless of how you want to live, I'll be right beside you. Because you're the sum of all these, and you're not separate from your past."

A happy ending is not my cup of tea

"Almost there," she says, I'll be with you in two months."

So, is everything we talked about and dreamed about going to be reality?"

"I've got a really tight schedule, sweetheart. I mean, we could see each other like that, you know. For a few minutes, at any old place."

"Look, you don't get it. I'd give up the world just to be with you another five minutes. Don't you worry about a thing, I arranged everything. Just tell me that we'll be able to check into the apartment around two in the afternoon. What time do you want to check out in the evening?"

"Five thirty, six... Is that enough?"

"Hmm, actually we could stay until the morning."

"Are we going to drink wine?"

"Sure, of course, why not."

"Then are we going to sleep together?"

"I'd really like that, but you know I enjoy sleeping alone. No problem, there's more than one bed in the room."

"That's not necessary."

"I don't get it."

"I'm saying, fine. Night, wine and a single bed."

"Are you serious?"

"Yes."

"I love you very much."

"Don't love me. Then again, keep talking that way with me. Like before, you and me. Don't tell me you love me. I hate that stuff. I

don't want to turn this into a regular relationship."

"Fine... Good night."

"Good night to you, my dear."

After closing the chat window, I immediately deleted my browsing history, because I really enjoy deleting my past. After turning on
Mozart's Requiem, I turned off the room light. I
then turned the computer armchair to the side
and plopped my legs onto my bed. Then I leaned
way back and closed my eyes. I clasped my
hands behind my head and slowly began to
move my shoulders left to right. Nora hates
Mozart, which is why I listen to Mozart at full
volume whenever I want to be alone, which is
most of the time. I listen to Maria Callas and
Emma Shapplin, who are still alive. I love
Emma's duet with George Dalaras, I must've
watched him hundreds of times. I never miss the
moment Emma Shapplin looks admirably at
Dalara, because I hate the admiration people
have for each other. If you ask me, nobody

should be amazed by somebody else's success in a field of interest. Again, I think whoever works hard on whatever subject can definitely rise to the top in that subject. This is not something to be admired, why should people be separated between those who have admiration and those who are admired? After mulling this over, I started to move my fingers as if I was conducting an orchestra without opening my eyes because I know how to use my fingers well. My fingers are passionate—you can't even imagine what symphonies they can create when they combine with the conductor in my mind. It doesn't matter whether there's anybody else in the room, seeing is believing. There's just no stopping my fingers and the conductor in my mind, as I'm a totally different person. For instance, just today, I created a stupid reason to stop myself from continuing with her. I'm in the dark in my room with the door and windows shut now, and if you see how I feed my mind with my Requiem and my passionate fingers, you'll understand how I slowly ascend in my room from the armchair to the ceiling, while listening to divine hymns in my ears. I don't enjoy being happy because in my opinion, people shouldn't be happy, I mean, what happiness is this? What's the admiration for these poor folks all about, when I shouldn't even be happy? I hate people who admire people, again today, as I extend my arms forward and am going over towards the window now. I told her not to say I love you, don't tell me today that you love me because if you do, it means you can love someone else too, that you love me or after me...

A few days later

She's uploaded new photos. Isn't that just swell? She looks great, healthy. With her friends, outside. She's smiling, she doesn't look sad. I wonder if she decided to back away from me. And why so quickly? Damn, she's got a lot of friends, she's so vivacious! Full and pro-grammed, like her entire life was programmed, with my parts that just need some drastic rear-ranging. As for me, I'm going to complete my evolution by slowly rotting away, by being afraid of my own shadow, and becoming smellier by the day.

30 years ago

I was young, very young and everything was going quite well for me. I guess that's something unexpected from a country like ours. I wasn't even 20 years old, and I was managing a pretty chic eatery in a dark corner of the city. If I said pretty chic, I mean really chic. I didn't stop at home, I was getting by with a few hours of sleep per day. My customers were an odd lot. Mostly whores of all nationalities. There were also revolutionaries, filling a table with their big beards and whispering and jotting down notes until evening. Youngsters of the 'hood filled another table. They were unemployed, broke, straight kids. The cops would come and go, peering the tables through the corner of their eyes. The whole precinct knew me anyway, I was summoned once a week for something or another; who was that, who was this, who was he talking to, what were they talking about and so on. Lovers of the women used to sometimes come by, or else their husbands. Tables and chairs would be tossed into the air like matchsticks. They'd pump the place up with obscenities, threats, and even lead. Those were the good ol' days. Some of the whores, and girls from the 'hood would fall in love with me, I wasn't that bad lookin', if you know what I mean. I was trying to love them back as much as I could.

At some point in time, some freak by the name of Nhamo had dropped into our cafeteria, someone from the dark continent. Chocolate, to put it kindly. One day she came stumbling in again, covered in filth. Inside there was incredible smoke. She came from between the table over to me, smacking into the kids as he went. I swear her stench was going to blow my nose off. I said, "Nhamo, you should wash up once in a while, honey." She didn't care. She hastily pulled a few stones out of her coat pocket and after shaking them up in her palm, she scattered them all on my table. After leaning her coal-black head towards me, and examining the stones carefully, she took my hand in her palm. After looking intently at it with her huge eyes, she said,

"You've got a lot of troublesome years waiting for you." After scrutinizing the lifelines in my palm, she went on, "After those years, and when you have completely lost all hope, a great reward awaits you."

"Nhamo", I repeated, "You disappointed me. What trouble, my chocolate? Everything's going just fine."

After hearing this, she turned her eyes from my hand to my face and said, "Yes, yes!" She said, "This reward is your sweet chocolate. She'll set everything right for you."

Who are you?

My grandmother raised me. I spent my childhood with her. She was a very cultured and disciplined woman. She'd say, "My baby, you definitely need to be nourished with other things besides your education." I was still quite small. "It could be music, literature, it could be theater. It doesn't matter, but it should be something."

Would you believe I was using a knife at dinner when I was just three years old. I received singing lessons when I was five and violin lessons when I was six. I was enrolled at the finest schools. By the time I was seventeen, I had wandered through most of the European capitals. I graduated from the French Language and Literature Department, with a second degree in Interpretation and Translation.

I married shortly after my grandmother died. I guess I wanted to fill the void she left behind. Nevertheless, our marriage turned into a nightmare during the first few months. I had married before we really got to know each other and then he showed me his true colors. *We broke up.*

You had an injured baby seagull in your hands when we first met at the pharmacy, where I had gone in to buy some anti-depressant medicine I'd been using for the past couple of months. You were telling the lady behind the counter,

"This seagull came running into my shop and I had a tough time kicking out the cats chasing it. What should I do with it?"

Just then, I experienced an involuntary fit of laughter. You were just standing there with a seagull in your hand and you didn't know what to do with it. "Goofy." I said to myself. "This boy is goofy!" I waited. Then I watched you. I was behind you as you returned to your shop with the seagull. I was still laughing because you had yet to figure out where to leave it. First, you put it on top of a table, then you picked it up and left it on the ground. Then you put it back on the table. If I hadn't used my head and brought you a cardboard box, you probably would have dawdled like that until evening.

While waiting···

I was tracking her social media accounts. She hadn't added anything new since that day. Whats up with that?

She had said, "I had a point of darkness. You touched a nerve."

How did we first meet?

It was as if a bird had entered the shop, and I was thinking about what to do with it, when she suddenly appeared behind me, holding a cardboard cookie box,

"Excuse me, but I was wondering if this box would be of any use to you?"

When did this happen, 10 years ago, or maybe even more?

I thanked her and took the box from her, I think she was laughing at me.

She came around again a few days later while I was reading a book at my table. I didn't remember her at first, and I wouldn't have remembered her if she hadn't asked about the bird. She was a petite, cute, nice, girl, very young.

Later on, practically every day, she'd come around to the cafeteria, sit across from me and lay everything on the line, books, films, soap operas, her stories, my stories...

After chatting for a bit, I was obliged to shut her up saying I had work to do.

This was happening towards the end of the brilliant years when my books were published one after another, when I received awards, my business went well, and love and bottles dizzily danced day and night around my head.

I was actually tired to death without even realizing it.

Fine, so who are you?

I've been around here for you this long, but it's like I've known you for much longer. You're very quiet. I'm trying to get close to you, but you don't notice me. Darling, there's an invisible wall between us, did you put it up, or was it put up for you, darling? Why don't you look in my face? Why don't you try to get to know me. You're constantly coughing. Are you sure you're alright? You look exhausted. What's tiring you? Why don't you get some rest?

I have to go soon. Is there anything you want to say?

We're going to get together again when the day comes. My points of darkness, your mysterious airs, your fears. We need to evolve and we need to defeat them now in order to overcome them. We have things to experience, to see, to acquire beforehand. This is not all we are, because we have a lot more inside us and it will always be there. The years we spend and the suffering we experience are going to bring us closer to each other as the days go by. The things that disappoint you, the things you fear won't happen, these won't be with us. We will come back stronger, and we'll improve each other.

What do you want?

"I'm thinking of you." Why did she write this? Does she want to drag this on, aren't I tired of all this stuff, doesn't she understand? She's a really young girl, clean as a whistle. But doesn't she see I'm so weak that I can barely stand on my feet? Didn't I just recently emerge from the hell of what she wants to experience, so how can I bring anyone closer to myself so easily?

I'm glad she left without me saying anything to her.

Many beautiful, long years await you. What do you want with a wreck like me? Look, you might've had some unpleasant experiences, and that's natural. Time doesn't always pass with love and happiness. Just let yourself go with the flow. "You'll learn and get stronger as you grow." Life will be as good as you can hold it in your hand. When in fact we just broke up yesterday. Yesterday, the day before, the day before that... They are gone, I stayed, but it's definitely not a victory. Nothing's going to be the same for me anymore.

The Sanatorium

(second dream)

"Knock off that damn racket!" he shouted inwardly from where he laid in his dream.

"They're crying from hunger," replied the woman desperately, "There's nothing left we can feed them."

The man pulls the blanket over his head. After tossing and turning a bit, he gets out of bed, muttering. He quickly enters the kitchen, opens the cabinet, looks in the drawers, and rummages through the shelves. Nothing!

There's nothing at all. He throws on his beat up coat and goes out of the door. It's cold and snowy outside. He rummages through the snow-covered trashcans. He digs out a half-eaten savory roll and a moldy crust of bread and devours them on the spot. Then he goes onto the avenue. One by one, he enters the shops lined up in a row, without compunction. He wants a job. Just to fill his belly, or even half his belly, but to no avail. "There's no work," they say.

It's not wartime, there's no drought or famine, he's not in the countryside, but there's no work and the man's hungry and his family's hungry. You've got to have a job or else there's no money, if there's no money, there's no heating for the flat, if there's no heating, there's no food—There's no living either.

He walks on, going in and out of the shops. He finds some scrub wood on the ground and throws it in a plastic bag. It'll be fuel for the stove at night, so the kids don't catch cold and get ill. Getting ill is another disaster entirely. There's no social security, there's no money, If you don't have it, you don't get treated and you can't buy medicine, too. Death is the illness of the impoverished.

A man saunters by him, shouting at the top of his voice;

"They're selling Cyprus! So why did we sacrifice all those martyrs 30 years ago? For whom did their blood flow, why did those young lives go there? Allah is on the side of the oppressed! Allah is going to have both sides account for this! Hey my Moslem brethren, believe and trust in Allah, He protects those who believe, he protects the oppressed!"

People are applauding him.

The man ruffles through the garbage bins, dumps the food remnants he finds into a bag to take home and puts the scrub in another bag. He asks for assistance from passersby, "Help." Nobody turns around to look at him. Everyone's running pell-mell. People are passing him, vehicles are passing him, street vendors are passing him, everyone's in motion.

"Help."

The man's head turns, someone's honking their horn; "Are you crazy, man? Get the hell out of the middle of the street!"

"Help."

He goes back home. He goes in front of the stove, tosses the scrub into it and sets it alight. The children are crying, they're still crying. He hands the woman the bag. The woman sniffs the contents and grimaces,

"This is garbage, I won't feed garbage to my children!"

"Eating garbage is better than dying," says the man.

There's no water, there's no oil, there's no propane gas tank. There's nothing in the flat. Life goes on, but it's all outside. Everyone continues going on their merry way, as all their feet and tires are constantly moving. The guy thrusts his head out of the window,

"What's going on?"

"Where you going?"

"Why aren't you stopping?

"Why don't you see us?"

"We're here."

"We're dying!"

The steps get more frequent, colors change as it gets dark outside. The children are crying and shaking. The man looks for the woman. The woman is lying face down on the bed, sobbing quietly. She soon gets up, takes her children in her bosom and adamantly walks towards the door.

"Where are you going?"

The woman doesn't reply as she goes out, pulling the door shut behind her. She's trembling as she walks onto the street with her children. She jumps in front of passersby, "They're starving, help us."

People are avoiding her, as they move quickly away.

"You can't trust anyone."

"The world's full of liars."

"She's probably richer than us."

"It's easy to beg, why don't you work like us!"

"Are we begging?"

"What a shame, isn't it?"

"You're too young to be doing this!"

"You should be ashamed of yourself!"

Words fly in the air.

All eyes are upon her, everyone's yelling at her. The children are crying.

"You're guilty!"

"You shouldn't have brought them into the world!"

The streets judge the woman, people are swearing at her, despising life.

"Yes. This woman!"

"You're the guilty party!"

The woman's running left and right. She's asking for help from everyone and everything and the same man is passing in front of her now,

"Turkish soldiers won't be living shields for US troops! Hey American lackeys, Hey infidels! Allah is going to hold you to account for this! You're going to pay the price on both sides! Hey Moslem ummah! Have faith in Allah. Trust Him and pray for Him. He protects us all!"

People are applauding him.

Two young men approach the woman, saying, "Come to our place, we've got plenty of food and booze."

The woman tries to get away from them. They have grabbed her by the arms and are trying to drag her. The woman sticks herself tighter to her children, who are crying.

"C'mon. Don't be coy."

The woman's miserable, hungry, tired and cold. She goes back home. Her man's in bed, his eyes are shut and he's smiling. There's a knock on the door. The woman opens the door with the hope of assistance or a plate of food. It's the landlord. He wants his rent money. He's ranting and raving.

"Get outta my flat!"

"Vacate the premises!"

"How dare you!"

"You got no scruples!"

The woman shuts the door. She draws the curtains shut rigorously and turns off the lights. The man is still grinning in his dream. The woman goes into the bathroom and collapses to her knees on the tiles. She clamps her hands

over her ears. She still hears her children sobbing, she hears the car horns honking, she hears
the people's chuckling. She shuts her ears
tighter, even tighter, and tighter still! She presses
her head on the tiles. The sounds suddenly cut
out. A shepherd is blowing a wooden flute and a
child is singing a melody. They also go silent
shortly. There is no sound coming. The woman
is motionless. There's an unfathomable silence
and fear. The children are no longer crying, and
the cars are no longer passing.

War is over. Life is over.

From behind a window in the distance,
the sobs of another child begins reverberating
down the dark streets.

His mother is about to take him into her
lap and try to console him. Then another coarse
male voice is going to be heard,

"Knock off that goddamned racket!"

In my city

Business had slowly started to get back on track after I returned from Istanbul. I stopped taking medication and started meeting up with my old friends. I decided to learn Hebrew. I started taking on translation jobs again. As all the works of my favorite writers had been translated and published before, I went in pursuit of new writers. I translated books I determined had not been translated into Turkish and sent them to the publishers. A few of them were published. I was wondering if you knew about this or not. I thought you'd appreciate it if you were informed. That's because we had stopped writing to each other. Our last dialogue went something like this,

"I came down with tuberculosis."

"You need to get some serious rest now."

I was getting little sleep and working a lot. I had no complaints. I developed a passion for astrology, and was opening a new star-chart for us every six months. Should I have contacted him? Response was always the same—No.

Coming Home

I emerged from the sanatorium with Nora after a six-month stint and we hailed a taxi to go home. It was nobody but Nora and I. My relationship with my family had left a lot to be desired and besides, I wasn't someone who was sought after in that type of environment. That's why my illness didn't garner much attention from anyone. We took pains not to talk more than necessary and come eye-to-eye with anyone. With the idea of serving as an example for those around me, we fell for the sake of youth and married, even though I hated the institution of marriage. Nothing ever good came to mind whenever marriage was mentioned. The life I lived was not at all suitable for this. When I found out I was ill, I didn't think I'd ever return, so I sold my interest in the shop for next to nothing. It was obvious a new and painful period was awaiting me. No doubt Nora was aware of this. I have lived by the seat of my pants for years, I accumulated no savings, and I didn't have a diploma that was worth anything. Having smiled down at me when I was young, Lady Luck got me riled up to bring me this far, but now what?

Home Alone

We must've been home for quite some time now. I had never looked so carefully at my bachelor pad. I lived alone for a while, then settled my family and went into the military. When I returned 18 months later, I moved my family to another house and got married. We've been here since then but I haven't spent much time inside. It was old when I bought it. Just as I hadn't been a good husband for Nora, I hadn't been a good owner to the house. The walls, ceilings, windowsills are tired, all the household items are worn out, the rooms smell moldy...

Does Nora want to continue with me despite everything? Or is she teaching me a lesson like, 'Who besides me is with you in these circumstances? There's nothing binding her, we didn't have children, we kept putting it off. She can move back in with her family if she wants. I mean, she doesn't have to stay with me.

I don't feel good, what with all the drugs, treatment, health checks, obligatory separation from old habits. My mind is far from its former brilliance, so is my age. What am I going to do?

New Era

I got married, without mulling over it too much. He's a publisher. We have a lot of common interests and it's going fine. You can call him handsome and successful as well. He's very sensitive and always understanding. We help, support and correct each other's work. A harmonious union. He doesn't get involved in my private life, I'm completely free. He's not like the other one, I was strangled.

I stopped looking at the night sky map as it doesn't occupy my mind like it used to. I have a straight lifestyle, and a decent social life as well. I started drinking booze, while accompanying him and his friends. There's somebody over at our place every night; writers, poets, critics, friends... Yes, it's going well for now.

Starting Over

I wanted to do something myself again first, to be my own boss in order to be free again. I visited my old friends and relatives for support, to no avail. I wasn't even aware we had distanced ourselves from each other and our relationship was getting colder. Nora was right, and it looked like Nhamo was on the verge of being justified. Then I started looking for work, which was quite humiliating. "What is your previous work experience, what's your scholastic career, what references can you show us?"

I was leaving home in the morning and coming back towards the evening with nothing to show for myself. I was in a funk and wasn't talking much with Nora and we tried not to make eye contact. I guess we didn't have much money, ditto for our friends as well. The days were passing in mundane succession.

What are you looking for?

The same circumstances, the same people, the same debauchery day in and day out started to get dreadfully boring after a few months. I had begun not to tolerate it and started losing touch with business and having insomnia. All the terrible headaches, arguments and the making up afterwards. I just couldn't go on like that. I told him I wasn't going to accept guests at home and alcohol wasn't going to be a part of the picture from that evening onwards. He acceded and we started anew.

For a while, I mulled it over in my mind again and I opened the map of the heavens. Should I have contacted him?

No.

The first dream in the house

I saw you first, dimly. I immediately remembered your face. You're facing me, standing
somewhere quite far from me. You're wearing a
short white dress, and you're much shorter than
me. Then I see myself. I'm naked. I'm standing
where I'm at, facing you. According to the spot
I'm looking at, I see my own back and the back
of my head, I have no legs, I don't see them. The
place where I am is darker and my surroundings
are completely empty. As for where you're at,
it's semi-illuminated, it's not tranquil illumina-
tion.. We've stretched our arms towards each
other. Our fingers are on the verge of touching,
but they just can't do so for some reason. Your
arm is proportional to your size, but mine is way
too long. First, I am checking out my surroundings. I'm peaceful, calm. Then I look intently towards you. As I look, a lot of heads appear
around your head—just heads, but tiny heads,

no bodies. These are tiny human heads that move like microbes. Some try to penetrate you through your ear, some through your mouth, some through your torso. They appear briefly, then disappear. I feel my tranquility has been ruined. My hands slowly retract into my arms, while yours just stay where they are. I discern sadness on your face. Or perhaps not? I can't be sure. My body in the dream is turning towards myself as we're intertwining and uniting. Then I look towards you again. There is consternation in my looks and a bit of anger as well. With your head half bent to the right, your lips are contorted, as you look towards me your hands slowly retract. Then I step out of view. The spot where you're at gets brighter the moment I disappear and a rough noise rises in the space. The number of heads rapidly increases, as dozens of heads are all around you. I can only see the upper part of your hair amongst the heads. Dark coffee. I suddenly think of Nhamo, the soothsayer woman from the cafeteria. My mind gets confused—dark coffee, chocolate, sweet chocolate. I suddenly get the urge to go back and see you again, but I can't. I force myself, and I feel like it'll happen the more I force myself. Just when I'm on the verge of seeing you, you disappear as the heads nibble away at you. We're losing each other. I wake up tired, in a cold sweat. Blind darkness of the night, naked on the bed and all alone. I'm thinking of you.

Talking with Nora

You know, I'd been looking for a job for a few months now, but I haven't found anything yet. I don't know because you managed, but we mustn't have had very much money left, and perhaps it had run out completely. I was never someone who knows how to be frugal. From now on I'll be earning less money than before, just a salary. We don't have any rent problems, although we shouldn't have any debts, nor do we have any children. We can manage, but you don't have to continue with me under these circumstances. We met when we were very young, we loved each other and got married. You loved that man you first knew—he was hardworking, talented and successful. I changed as I got older, in fact, I changed a lot. On the other hand, you've always remained the same, you've never changed, in fact, you're like you were on the first day. I really don't know which one's better. The distance between us grew wider and wider, I'm saying this in terms of direction. There's nothing I can promise you, more than you see. You can go back to your family if you want, and maybe you can get married again. You're still young and quite beautiful. You were always beautiful, gorgeous, good and faithful. The problem was me, I was the selfish, arrogant one. I was looking down on everything and I thought it would go on like this. It didn't happen. I was slapped around the head. I don't think I'll ever have the opportunity to continue my old lifestyle again. I don't think I would enjoy that kind of lifestyle either. That's why I want you to think it out carefully and make the right decision for yourself. Honestly, I should never have married in the first place but, as I said, I wasn't equipped to realize that at the time. Don't think of me while making your decision, I can take care of myself, in fact, I've always looked after myself. I've been working since my childhood, I've been involved in various jobs and I've also been successful. Now, the situation is different but I still think I've got enough experience to take care of myself, but nothing more.

After listening to my discourse in her armchair without a single interruption, she laid it on the line without compunction,

"I'm staying with you."

Nora

When I first laid eyes on you, you were smoking a cigarette next to the door of your store, with your back up against the wall. Even though it was so long ago, I remember it like yesterday. That's because it was not a moment I could easily forget. You were standing and staring at me wearing a simple black T-shirt and tight jeans below. I realized I was your destiny the very moment our gaze met. If it was possible to relive that moment, I would've liked to change your destiny. Except for the first few years, I know you weren't happy enough living with me. I've always remained the same towards you, but you've changed a lot. Imagine a woman who loves what she wrote and who understands her soul better than me, wandering inside this house in my place. Time passed nicely for you and her, isn't that right? Until this age, you lived a beautiful life that satiated you and you should be grateful for that. Your world of emotions, which has finally reached an intensity that you can't cope with, rendered you weak and sick. I know there have been many women in your life, I know. They were momentary lapses of reason, one-night stands or something a little more serious. Different women loved you in every period of your life, depending on your work tempo, and you loved them back without caring too much. You also had serious relationships that lasted longer. I was sad, but I didn't let you onto it and, despite everything, I never did anything to upset you. Maybe you wouldn't be upset, I don't know, but I just didn't. You turned out to a very difficult dilemma and disappointment for me, but I always continued. At the start of your illness, I heard the names of many women come out of your mouth while you tossed and turned, sweating profusely at night in bed, and I never mentioned them to you. You seemed very weak and in need of care and there wasn't anybody else but me at your side. I couldn't leave you like that. You asked once and I answered without hesitating,

"I'm staying with you."

Where are you?

He's changed. He can't rid himself of his alcohol problem. He comes home drunk very late while I'm asleep. He's started interrogating me and doesn't give me any breathing space. Why did you say that, why did you write like that, who's that who's this... He's probing my every action, my every sentence, trying to find other meanings under it all. I'm suffocating. I'm not used to this. I have invested a lot of time and effort in myself and I'm happy as I am. I'm not going to try to change myself for him or anyone else. It can't go on like this, because I can't continue if I'm not happy. I can't go on even if I love him or if I'm in love.

I miss him.

He got ill, and we hadn't written to each other since then. Was he able to recover? What's he got that attracts me to him this much, even in his absence? I wonder if he's also thinking of me? I don't think so, as I hadn't received any such vibe from him. So why did he write me when he got ill? I told him to call a friend of mine in Istanbul who can come by and see how he's doing. The cafeteria was sold, and it's under new management. He had no news about this. Where are you?

1100 kilometers away

I'm wandering through the streets, like a loiterer. I'm not even sure I'm really looking for a job, I seem to be wasting time aimlessly. For some strange reason, my father unexpectedly comes to mind these days as I pass a building, or a shop. Did he feed me some dessert here when I was small, did he buy a toy from there, or did we get on that ferry and cross over to the other side?

I didn't know him very well, I guess I didn't want to know him. He was a decent artisan, an alcoholic. *He was born in 1931. I don't know much else about him. That's because I left home when I was still a kid and went my own way. He also did the same, but he was 13 years old when he travelled 1100 kilometers to Istanbul.*

Once, when I was little, he took me to where he came from and introduced me to our relatives. It was a very crowded family that lived on a long, narrow street, which comprised of interconnecting single-storey homes surrounded by a central courtyard. There was a loving, crowded family in every house. The tops of the homes were open to the elements, like sky terraces with mosquito nets. It was a nice, big family that slept beneath the stars. I was delighted and felt I belonged there. This was about 35 years ago, maybe more, I never went back there again after that.

Home Life

He started work. He works for a small insurance agency on a back street of a nearby neighborhood. He gets there early in the morning and comes straight home in the evening. He doesn't drink, he hasn't started smoking again, at least not yet. I don't know why, but he goes on foot every day. He carries no cash in his pocket, and brings his entire salary to me. He eats dinner when he returns home and then goes to bed and sleeps. He's impotent. There's no trace of his old days. He's long gone when I get up in the morning. He doesn't converse with anyone and doesn't carry a phone. He stopped writing, he's not reading books or anything anymore. Television's never been his thing since way back when. Time goes by like this. He's not happy, but he's got no complaints either. He's quiet.

The other night, he was really surprised when I asked, "Shall we make a kid?" He was like this had never occurred to him until now. I said, "I'm asking because it's getting near the end of my biological cycle."

After mulling it over for a bit, he replied, "I don't want one, what about you?"

"It doesn't matter," I said. I never brought up the topic again.

Sweet Chocolate

I separated from my second husband. After mauling each other as bitterly as we could, we finished it off completely, period. I'm beat. After two marriages and two separations at this age, my only consolation was not having a child, thank goodness. How am I going to pick up the pieces? There's almost nothing left that I enjoy. I'm seriously considering a move to another city to start a new life. Will I be able to manage?

Nowadays, I feel like writing to him to explain what's been happening, to share my problems, and to perhaps get a little close to him. I wish...

At His Workplace

I think I've turned over two years, and I'm managing to hang in there. I come in the morning and open the office before everyone shows up. I try not to think anything about the past in order to maintain a calm, healthy mind. It's not easy, but at least I'm trying.

First, I clean up in the office, wiping down the tables and dusting off the peripherals. Then I load up on whatever paperwork there may be. I'm trying not to leave my mind empty for even a single moment. One day, sweet chocolate popped into my mind again when I was in a good mood. I sent her a message. I wanted her to know I was fine. It was short, but sometimes that I think of her, for some inexplicable reason. My e-mail was returned, with a note saying her mail account was deactivated. I was sorry.

Nora has spruced up the flat with the money left over after expenses. Repairs, paint, new furniture, etc.

I walk nearly 10 kilometers a day, and get a kick out of doing so. I was getting tired in the beginning, but now I think nothing of it, and I'm quite used to it. I try controlling my diseased mind while walking, but there are times when I can't help ask myself. What is a person? I ponder my old life a little, and then the new one. Let's say, they're going to ask after leaving this mortal soul,

"What did you do?"

Answer, "I worked for a private insurance company in a commercial office in Sirkeci, and came here right after I retired."

If it was me, I would've said, "Wow, how about that shit, now do yourself a favor, turn around and get the hell out of here!"

Solar Turn

It's been two years since I divorced, and I'm alone. I postponed my plans to move to Istanbul or another city. As time passes, everything that happened is forgotten because there's no trace left. The thoughts I once had of leaving the city had lost their validity. While I try not to dwell on all of that, I sometimes can't help but ask myself, "What's time?" Then he creeps back into my mind—What's he doing these days?

I opened my solar return map, first mine. Is there any return from someone in the past?

Minutes pass interminably, I'm curious:

No···

Then I opened his map, I had already learned his birthday, his birthplace and the exact time.

"Health, work, daily life."

None of this was along his lines...

He has a pessimistic future outlook. He's thinking of the past but he also can't go back to somebody in his past.

I'm going to continue waiting for the right time.

Dreaming of Chocolate

From Eden[*]

I'm sprinting stark raving naked through a desolate forest at night. The tune, *'From Eden'* is ringing in my ears:

Babe, there's something tragic about you
Something so magic about you

As I run and as the lyrics echo in the forest, predators appear and start running alongside me, for no apparent reason.

I suddenly realize that I'm searching for you. I stop. Then I shout as loud as I can, "I'm running naked at night in a desolate forest, darling, where are you?"

---

[*] 'From Eden' - Hozier

Animals hear my shouting also move into action—horses are neighing, bears are muttering, wolves are howling as we continue running deep into the forest. Our song continues to play, as well,

> *'Babe, there's something lonesome about you. Something so wholesome about you Get closer to me"*

I see you later. Here you are, at the bottom of a deep pit. I'm calling out to you while bending my head down and holding it, "Darling, I'm here, I'm here" You don't hear me...

Our song continues to reverberate in the forest, in tempo with the howling wolves.

> *'Babe, there's something wretched about this. Something so precious about this. Oh what a sin"*

You're not moving, your arms are tied to your legs, you're heads out in front of yourself, and you're sitting in silence. It's like you're dwelling upon something. I'm hopelessly accompanying the last verse of the song with my lips.

'I slithered here from Eden just to hide outside your door"

I'm sweating profusely as I awake, more tired than ever. I'm naked on the bed and I'm alone on a moonless, dark night. I'm thinking of you.

Chocolate's Birthday

It was her birthday today, everyone's celebrating it on her page. It says she's turned 30, when in fact she doesn't look it at all. She always looks like she's a university co-ed. Her page's filled with hearts, goblets, and flowers, and of course, all are paintings. We hadn't written to each other in a month, this time I wanted to break the ice. I don't want to lose her, but I guess I don't want to lose this balance even more, I mean, less, but always. Almost impulsively, I sent an official message celebrating her birthday. She answered immediately, polite but distant. As it was, our longest correspondence was on that day, I guess we kind of missed each other. It wasn't long to our rendezvous, and I'm excited and stressed out. She tries to get me to chill, and she succeeds.

From what I gather, she's read something like ten times more books than me, despite the age difference between us. It would be great if she only understood literature, but she also has a handle on cinema, as well as music. It's as if she grew up on the street of the fine arts... I'm stuck reading what she wrote on the screen, how opposite we are to each other. While I'm trying to discharge whatever is in my memory, she has been constantly filling her mind in pursuit of the trivial and not so trivial. Of course, what's deemed trivial and not so trivial is relative, because when it all comes down to it, there's a strong possibility I'm of the trivial persuasion.

Nora Is Stunned

He's in his forties, and he's started betting on the horses. Actually, he never had a notion about such things before. He doesn't even know how to play backgammon or card games... He'd come around every night with a newsletter in his hands and after dinner would retreat into his room and start his research. Bulletin scores, handicap scores, dosage profile, jockeys, origins...

His vision is so screwed up, he can't even make out the horses while watching the races on TV. He constantly changes tactics while filling in his race ticket. Some days he bets according to the names of the horses, some days according to the jockeys on the racing form, while other times, according to the numbers. In the end, it's all for naught, nada, nichivo. I know from my father, he spent his life chasing after the horses.

He used to head over to Veliefendi Hippodrome every Sunday when we were kids, and he'd take us with him if we wanted to. He started playing with the six-pack, then the five- and four-pack, and then ended the day with a single. I never saw him win once, on the contrary, he lost a ton of money at the races.

He wanted to earn a windfall and return to his previous life. He was going to open a cafeteria or perhaps a bar, depending on the amount. Those pipe dreams were all soon left by the wayside.

He doesn't make a big thing about it, but he most definitely missed his old lifestyle. He had his books, the awards, the women and girls who meandered within his radar range. Not to mention a morning drink, his most favorite thing since his youth. It didn't matter what time he went to bed at night, he'd wake up early the next morning and enjoy a drink, whether it was beer, wine or raki. Then, he'd go back to sleep and doze until noon. It's been nearly four years since he touched a drink or a cigarette.

He's been caught up with figures lately, and started talking to himself,

"Yesterday, the number 8 horses won three legs, and the number 5 horses won four legs the day before, which means the number 2 horses will win at least three legs today." It didn't wind up like that, nor had it for years. One day he pushed everything aside and filled in his coupon with just the numbers of his birthday: 1-2-1-2-6-9. That evening was the first and last time he guessed the six-pack. He won a minor prize, because all the winning horses were favorites. Nevertheless, for some reason, he didn't want to accept this. He was saying, "No, those horses were going to win if they were longshots instead of favorites. The problem isn't with the horses or jockeys."

Then what was the problem?

The Guy's Daydream

The years passed in quick succession with
the same monotony, and if you ask me, in the
same ineptitude. My retirement is right around
the corner. My hair and beard have all turned
white. I've recently started smoking again and
do so whenever I feel like it. There's something I
always think about, and that is the desire to
think. I say, settling down in a quiet, deserted,
faraway spot, at least in the final years of my
life, even it was just for a few years of more soli-
tude, of more thinking, but not thinking about
the past, this is something else. I mean, with bil-
lions of stars poised about my head, when the
universe is actually so ginormous and mysterious, I'd like to have my bare feet treading the
dirt, or perhaps be in a wooden hut, or maybe in
a tree house, just hanging out. Unfurnished,
without souvenirs, empty and silent. I just want
to ignore all this stuff and not to have to deal

with nonsensical stuff, unnecessary documents, stupid people, bills, etc. anymore. Without thinking of making income, business that is, without any feeling of the brunt of responsibility. I think this is all sheer stupidity when we're living under all these stars. Maybe writing another book, a light fiction with stars, numbers, thoughts, dreams and so on would set me back on track after all these years. It should be a magical love story with a happy ending because as of yet, I haven't written anything with a happy ending, and I think that we as writers must evolve.

Lest I confess, I'd want my sweet chocolate to come there by my side once in a while, to sit together beneath the stars. Then imbibe wine and tobacco together, without too much conversation. Her youth, her brilliance, her knowledge, her come-hither looks would do me a world of good.

Speaking of being beneath the stars, the place where my father took me in my childhood came to mind, the sky terraces with mosquito nets back home in the countryside.

I don't have the slightest hope about the future, or even the slightest clue.

For hell's sake, why am I still here?

The Combine

Ours is a connection that doesn't break, has no end and is always set up for us to get back, and we'll ultimately return to each other when the time comes. Even if we don't see each other for a long time, I know we'll come together one day.

Years later, I'll open the map and ask once more,

"Should I make contact with him?"

"Yes."

Finally···

There's a return to a relationship in the past... In fact, there's even reviving the art of penmanship.

The time has come ···

"I'm glad to see you again."

"I'm also very glad to see you again..."

The Writer's Narrative

Everything transpired just like the young woman, that is, sweet chocolate, had planned. Thirteen years after their first rendezvous, the man is rather excited and timid, while the woman is relaxed, strong and full of self-confidence. Through a joint decision, they met in front of the gate of the Old Train Station around 1 p.m. The man looked like he didn't know where to put his hands, let alone what to say, but these bore no importance, because she had thought this all out down to the finest details. Grinning, she slowly approached the man with the pink suitcase in her hand.

"Hi," she said sweetly, without frightening him. She left her travel bag on the ground, touched the man's arms with her petite hands and peered into his eyes. "You're fine, aren't you?" The man nodded his head affirmatively.

"Shall we go then if you're ready?" asked the young lady, as the man nodded his head again.

They got into a taxi waiting in front of the train station and got off in the city square. The man wanted to take the lady's suitcase from her hand but the sweet chocolate didn't even accede to that.

She said, "We still have some time before entering the flat, sweetheart. Shall we sit somewhere for a while?" The man nodded his head again. After leaving her suitcase next to a man sitting on a park bench, they went into the shop across the way to buy a beverage, then they headed back.

"Would you like a smoke? Perhaps it'll help calm you." The man turned to look straight in the girl's face, then he replied,

"That'll be great."

The woman removed a packet of smokes from her pocket she brought for him, took out a cigarette, lit it with her lighter, took a deep pull on it and then handed it to the man. Then she gazed at the face of the man holding the cigarette in one hand and a cardboard coffee cup in the other, as she smiled, feeling relieved.

They took the key from the concierge and entered the flat. There was a bathroom at the entrance, a small kitchen counter against the sidewall of the bathroom, an armchair next to the counter, a coffee table in front of that, and the bedroom to the side. After shutting the door, they both stood idly apart from each other for a while. The man removed his jacket, dropped it on the armchair and then sat down. The woman followed suit and, after removing her coat and dropping it on the chair, she sat demurely next to the man. They remained in silence like that in the armchair for a while. It wasn't long before the man slowly turned his head towards the sweet chocolate face and looked into her eyes. When their rapidly approaching lips merged, the slightest pain of the past was deleted from their minds. They then embarked on a long journey with the joy of children inside their bodies entrusted to souls. The trip lasted from that afternoon until five the next morning.. After their final, very intense coupling at five o'clock in the morning, the girl leaned her head against the man's bare chest and closed her satiated, peaceful eyes.

After saying, "I never would've imagined that reality could be better than any dream," the man closed his tired eyes.

Life resembles a story; it's not important how long the work is, what's important is that it has to be good.

-Seneca

A Brief Note From Sweet Chocolate

I have prepared for us a life as you imagine it to be, under the stars, in the land you say you feel you belong to. All you have to do is tell me the date so I'll come and pick you up when you're ready.

A Short Note for Nora

A life in the land I feel I belong to, beneath the stars, as I once imagined has been prepared for me. I'm going, never to return.

Return

"Why do you have just this one photo in your wallet, sweetheart?"

"This is the photograph of me the year my father died, in fact, he died on that very day."

"How old were you in this photo?"

"13."

"What year was that?"

"2000."

"How old was I in 2000?"

"Hmm, 31."

"So, how old are you now?"

"31."

"How many years ago did we meet?"

"13."

They had a good laugh.

After departing the aircraft, they got into the taxi in front of the queue with a license plate beginning with '31' and told the driver where to go. After the car drove off, the man asked,

"Are we going to have to make children?"
"No," replied sweet chocolate as she smiled.

"We won't need to do anything but love each other."

Also by Merih Günay

THE SEAGULLS WEDDING

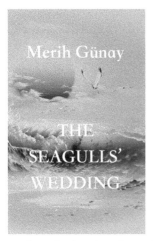 This short novel is set in the Istanbul of the 2000's, a world where the lives of ordinary law-abiding people are turned upside down by terrorism, earthquakes, wars and macro-economic financial crises. It is a world where people have forgotten to act like human beings and only look after themselves.

In the words of the hero himself, in the space of one month he has "lost his father, gone bankrupt, had his goods and chattels taken away from him, lost his home, been treated like a pervert, almost died of hunger and been abandoned by his family".

Our hero has opened a gift shop in the historic part of Istanbul, after years of hard, soul-destroying labour in hotels where he has been at the beck and call of unscrupulous, penny-pinching employers. The father he loses has spent most of his miserable life working long hours in similarly appalling conditions and the situation of the distant relative who pays him an unexpected visit and sees his abandoned, bankrupt state is little different.

Alienation and lovelessness are other underlying themes of this short novel. In it we see close family members who scarcely speak to each other, wives deserting their husbands and husbands deserting their wives and a funeral attended by a mere handful of people. There is ingratitude, too, in the actions of the hero as he pursues the beautiful Natalie, turning his back emotionally on her kindhearted but plain sister. Among the constantly recurring themes in "The Seagulls' Wedding" are the effects of privatization and government cuts on the lives of working men with families to support and the terrible guilt they feel when they cannot bring home enough money to pay the bills, a guilt which in some cases drives them to become vagrants. Children are forced to drop out of school and take up menial work just so that families can make ends meet.

Although the main character is somewhat unlikeable, this is an engaging story of his Don Quixote-like approach to life.

9 783949 197529